MW01011753

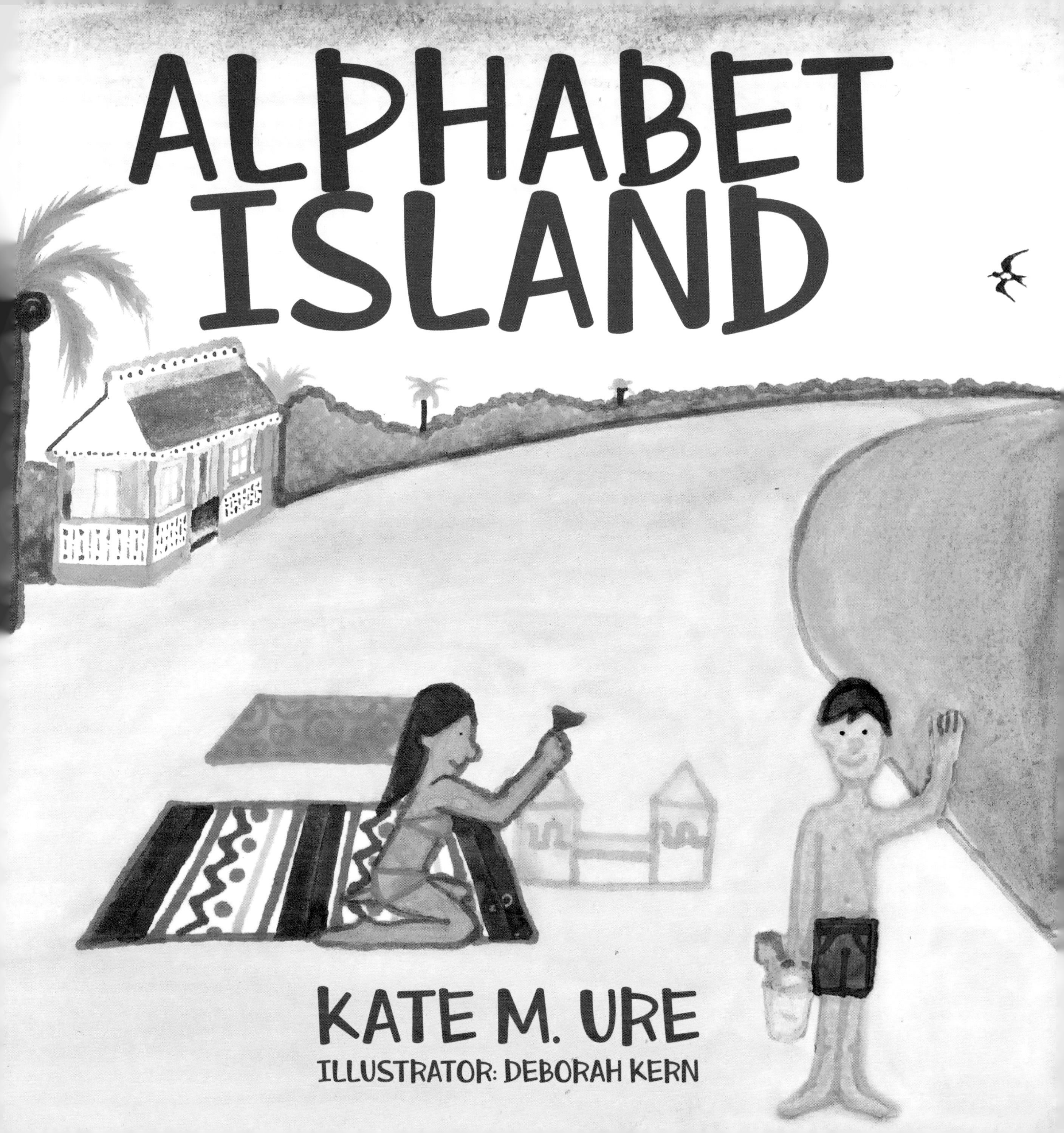
ALPHABET ISLAND
KATE M. URE
ILLUSTRATOR: DEBORAH KERN

DEDICATIONS

To island babies
everywhere, especially
"Diddy" and "Eleven."

– Kate

To Lily, you will always be
my island baby.

– Deborah

ALPHABET ISLAND

ISBN: 978-1-948074-00-1

Author: Kate M. Ure
Illustrator: Deborah Kern

Library of Congress Number in Progress

Published by CLM Publishing
www.clmpublishing.com
Grand Cayman, Cayman Islands

ePub: 978-1-948074-01-8
ePDF: 978-1-948074-02-5

Printed in the United States of America

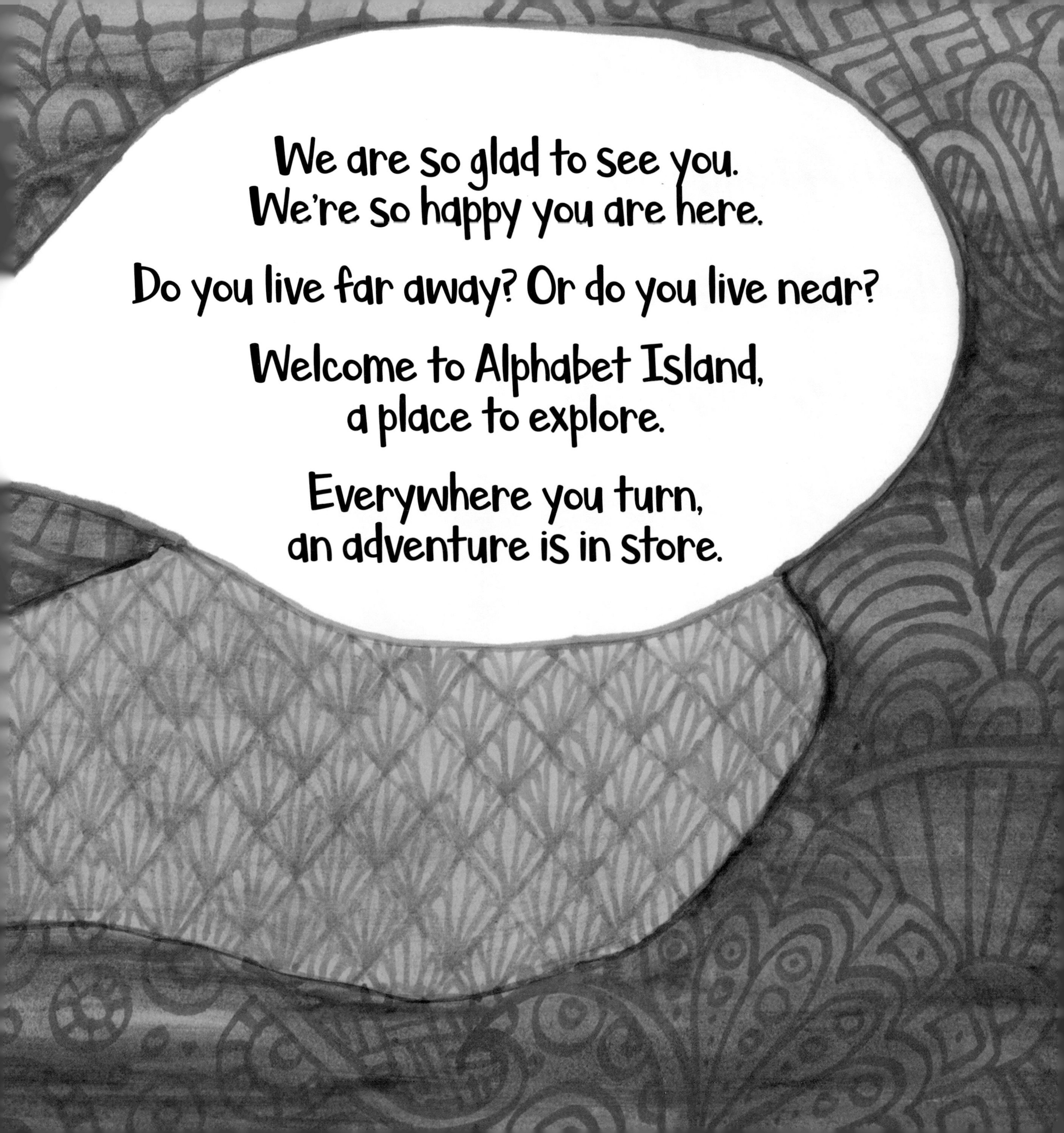

We are so glad to see you.
We're so happy you are here.

Do you live far away? Or do you live near?

Welcome to Alphabet Island,
a place to explore.

Everywhere you turn,
an adventure is in store.

You cannot get here by car, by bus,
or by train,

To explore Alphabet Island,
you must arrive by AIRPLANE;

Or ANCHOR a BOAT once you reach land,
And bury your toes in the BEACH's soft sand.

You can collect
CORAL jewelry
from the merchants'
beach huts,

OH NO! LOOK OUT!
Beware of falling
COCONUTS!

Above the water, DOLPHINS jump
and spin through the air.

Below the water, DIVERS breathe
from the tanks that they wear.

Ocean animals are enchanting;
their colors surreal.

Some blend in with their surroundings;

Some glow, like the ELECTRIC EEL.

FISH swim with their FAMILIES,
groups known as schools,
FROGS lay eggs under water which will
hatch into tadpoles!

Land animals are social,
like the GOAT who wanders free.

Can you spot the GRASSHOPPER and
GECKO settled in the tree?

The shelled HERMIT CRABS
burrow holes near the shore;

The HORSE and its rider gallop like musical décor.

The sun-loving IGUANAS
display their pointy, spiky
scales,

JELLYFISH have trailing tentacles that look like floating tails.

Hovering across water, KITESURFERS
ride the wind as they pass;

While underneath the surface,
LOBSTERS hide in tall sea grass.

A MANGO is a sweet treat.
The MERMAID basks beneath MOONBEAMS,
While navigating the open sea fills her
NAUTICAL dreams.

When the OCTOPUS gets scared
it releases a cloud of ink;

A PIRATE sits under a PALM tree
and sips a PAPAYA drink.

To unload the imported goods,
Barges use waterways called QUAYS,

At dawn, the ROOSTER'S "cock-a-doodle-doo"
is heard across the breeze.

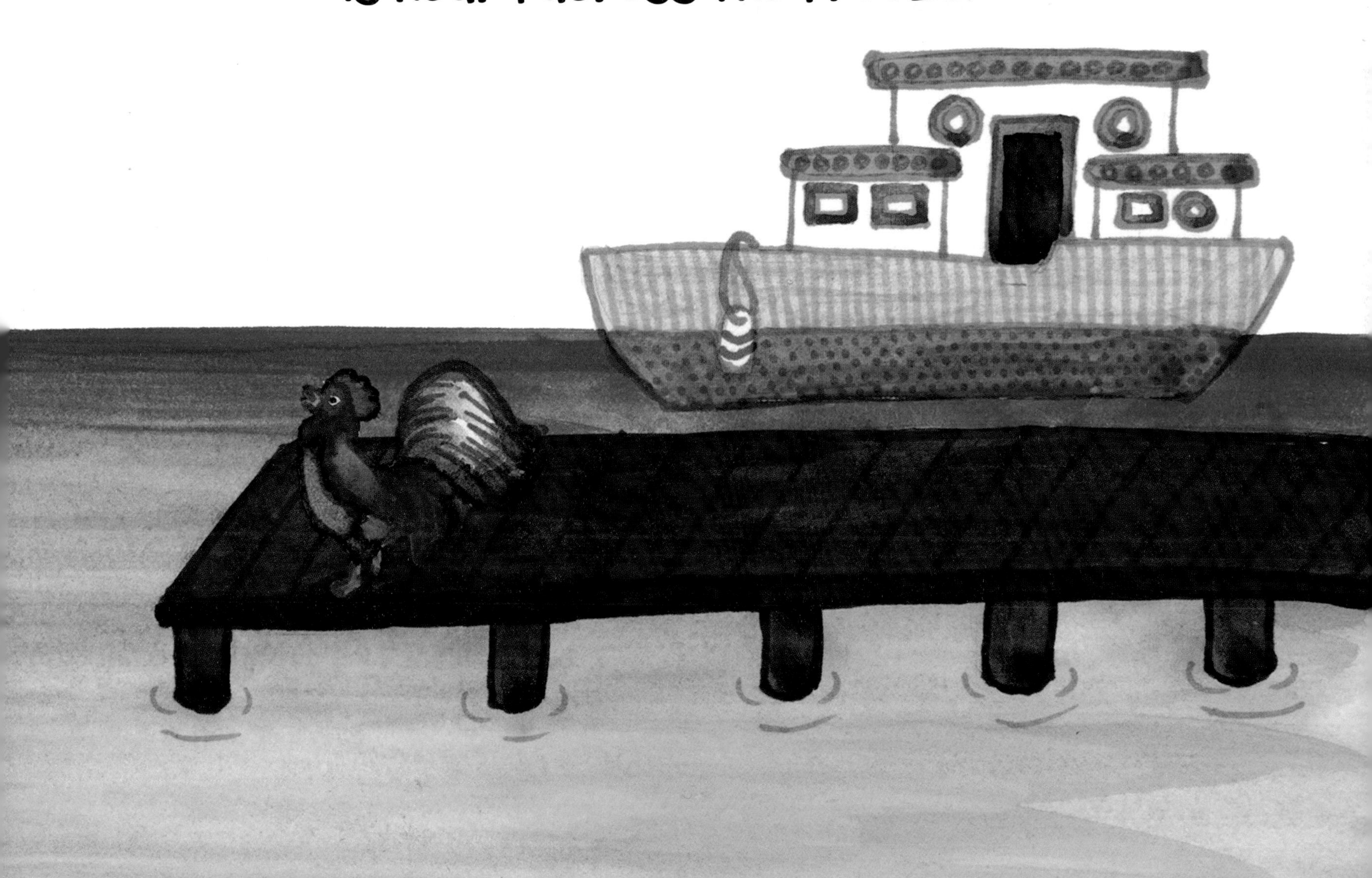

Gazing at the SUNSET, the SAILOR says,
"Thanks for shining bright."

Then sets his sights
on SHORE and SAILS his SAILBOAT
toward the night.

The SURFER catches a final wave
while gliding under the SWELL.

As night falls, STARFISH listen
to the tales that TURTLES tell.

Under an UMBRELLA, a man
strums a UKULELE tune,

Over the clouds, the VOLCANO erupts and roars a loud, “KA-BOOM!!”

Heard in the distance, the WATERFALL wails a thunderous splash,

As a pirate marks an "X" where his buried treasure is stashed.

Seen in the distance, YACHTS float proudly across the ocean.

As a ZIP LINER glides through the canopy with a swift and downward motion.

Alphabet Island
holds new adventures
each and every day.
We hope you enjoyed your visit,
Please come back soon to stay!

KATE M. URE, AUTHOR

Spending the first three decades of her life in Michigan and then Chicago, Kate took a leap of faith to trade in her winter boots for flip-flops and became an island dweller in 2011. She currently lives on Grand Cayman with her husband, two young daughters, and 90lb Goldendoodle named Jackson. In addition to writing her first children's book, Kate founded the wellness company KURE where she combines her expertise as a certified life coach, yoga instructor, Ayurveda advocate, and former women's health/obstetrics nurse educator. Her goal is to help women live "whole life" healthy. You can learn more about Kate at www.KUREliving.com or connect with her at kate@KUREliving.com.

DEBORAH KERN, ILLUSTRATOR

Originally from Lincolnshire in the United Kingdom, Deborah studied Animation at Staffordshire University, and did her Postgraduate Certificate in Education (PGCE) at Cambridge University. She has also lived in Washington D.C. and Naples, Italy before landing in the Cayman Islands in 2012, where she taught art at a public high school in Grand Cayman. Deborah and her husband have a big, crazy dog called Stanley, and, in the summer of 2017, welcomed a baby girl. She is also 1/3 owner of a modern ceramic collective called 3 Girls and a Kiln (3GK) creating beautifully customized ceramic pieces for individuals, hotels, restaurants, and galleries. You can take a look at what she has been up to at www.3girlsandakiln.com or connect with her at 3girlsandakiln@gmail.com